GLUCOSANITY

GlucoSanity
Copyright © 2023 by M.L. Kelly

Published in the United States of America
ISBN Paperback: 979-8-89091-009-7
ISBN eBook: 979-8-89091-010-3

All rights reserved. No part of this publication may be reproduced, stored in a retrieval system or transmitted in any way by any means, electronic, mechanical, photocopy, recording or otherwise without the prior permission of the author except as provided by USA copyright law.

The opinions expressed by the author are not necessarily those of ReadersMagnet, LLC.

ReadersMagnet, LLC
10620 Treena Street, Suite 230 | San Diego, California, 92131 USA
1.619. 354. 2643 | www.readersmagnet.com

Book design copyright © 2023 by ReadersMagnet, LLC. All rights reserved.

Cover design by Kent Gabutin
Interior design by Daniel Lopez

GLUCOSANITY

M.L. KELLY

Health  Diabetes

Choose Life   Breaking the Curse

Changing the Numbers
Of my Hemoglobin
AIC

The Success Is I'm the Blood

It can be done   That's the bottom line

To God Be The Glory!

DISCLAIMER / WARNING

Do not use this book or any of the contents to replace the services, guiding or treatment of any physician. Do not use it as a treatment for Diabetes. The information in this book is for your general knowledge, and is not a substitute for medical advice. Use the information at your own risk. Consult a physician before making any changes or using any of the information in this book.

A SPECIAL HONOR OF THANKS

I would like to take this time to give a deep heartfelt thank you to everyone who has loved and supported me, especially my family; my husband, may daughter, my son, my granddaughter and my friends. May God bless all of you exceedingly, abundantly, above all, that you can ask, dream, or believe.

Honors and Awards

- The Commanding General's Award (for outstanding volunteer service)
- The Pot of Gold Award – I volunteered at my son's elementary school in 1992.
- The Department of the Army Certificate of Appreciation (Wife of a U.S. Army Soldier)
- I supported my husband when he went to various wars in Kuwait, Iraq, etc. in 1993.
- Winn Army Community Hospital Certificate of Appreciation
- I gave flu shots in Practical Nursing School in 2000.
- Marquis Who's Who (Professional) iPad inducted in 2023
- I am a health screener and coach. I biometrically seen clients and coach them. I help them understand their results, answer their questions. I discuss their health goals, health histories, and I help them create a plan.

TABLE OF CONTENTS

To God Be The Glory v
Disclaimer / Warning vii
A Special Honor of Thanks ix
Honors and Awards xi
Introduction xvii

CHAPTER I	LISTENING TO THE HOLY SPIRIT, AND PRAYER 1	
CHAPTER II	THE DANIEL FAST 4	
CHAPTER III	.... 8 HEARING THE DIAGNOSIS OF TYPE II DIABETES FROM MY PHYSICIAN. LISTENING TO MY PRIMARY CARE ABOUT LABS, MEDICATION, WEIGHT LOSS ETC. (30 LBS. IN 3 OR 4 MONTHS) A FOLLOW-UP APPOINTMENT WAS MADE.	
CHAPTER IV	FEELINGS - SHOCK, OVERWHELMED, HOPEFUL 10	
CHAPTER V	A TRIP TO THE HEALTH FOOD STORE .... 11 WHEAT GRASS, KIDNEY & LIVER DETOX TEAS	

CHAPTER VI	TAKE EVERYTHING TO GOD IN PRAYERS	13

EATING, EXERCISE, BLOOD SUGARS (WHEN/ HOW OFTEN), WATER INTAKE, NUTRITIONAL SHAKES, READING BOOKS ABOUT DIABETES, PRAYING, TAKING COMMUNION AND WEIGHING MYSELF

CHAPTER VII	THE PLANS THE HOLY SPIRIT GAVE TO ME	16
CHAPTER VIII	MY JOURNAL	18

BLOOD SUGARS, DIET, WATER REGIMEN, LAB RESULTS, WEIGHT LOSS RESULTS, AND FINGER STICKS

CHAPTER IX	MY JOURNAL (DIARY)	21
CHAPTER X	THE END OF A JOURNEY/ BATTLE	23

WE WIN BECAUSE OF FAITH IN THE TRINITY GOD THE FATHER, GOD THE SON – JESUS, AND GOD THE HOLY SPIRIT.

CHAPTER XI	TIPS	24
CHAPTER XII	KEY POINTS	26
CHAPTER XIII	KNOWLEDGE	28

INTRODUCTION

FAITH LIKE

A mustard seed – mountain moving faith

If you have the faith of a mustard seed, you can say, mountain get out of my way, and the mountain will move. Jesus can heal anything. First, we have to believe that Jesus died on the cross to save us from our sins so that we can have everlasting life and get to know him as Jehovah Rophe "the Lord heals (our/ my) healer". Have a relationship with them – God the Father, God the Son (Jesus) and God the Holy Spirit. Talk to them, listen to them, and follow their instructions. Then you will have good success. Healing / Health / Wellness – I have known the Holy spirit since I was a little girl, so this wasn't my first time believing him. No, I haven't always talked, listened, and obeyed; but this time I did what the Holy Spirit told me – when you have faith like a mustard seed, and trust the Holy Spirit, he will be your fortress. He will be your refuge. In this book, I will talk to you about listening to the Holy Spirit, hearing the diagnosis of Diabetes from my Primary Care Physician, my feelings, a trip to the health food store taking everything to God in prayer, the plans the Holy Spirit gave to me, my journal, and the end of a journey/ battle. If you have the faith of a mustard seed, you can say, "The mountain gets out of my way, and the mountain will move."

CHAPTER 1

Listening to the Holy Spirit, and Prayer

Faith without work is dead.

I had faith (belief, trust, confidence, dependence, hope, reliance, and communion) in God. I believed in God. I trusted him. I had confidence in him and his word. I depended on him to help me identify activities (Listening to the Holy Spirit, prayer, exercise and listening to my physician) that helpedme to make changes. I had confidence that I would not be a diabetic after I went to my physician's office for an appointment to check my urine, blood pressure, pulse temperature, and FSBS Fasting Blood Sugar, and labs. I had to start exercising and making changes in my diet. I knew I could rely on the Holy Spirit. That kept me optimistic. I took my communion every morning. I talked to the Holy Spirit about my diagnosis of

Diabetes. Diabetes is not healthy. Every person is told the disease or condition can't be changed, but it can. I talked to the Holy Spirit about it. He said it could be changed. I could win my war against Diabetes with his help. I was relieved. Some people are given classes or information that tells them how to live with it or how to manage it. I worshiped God. I thought about doing everything I could to get a non-diabetic result. I prayed. The Holy Spirit gave me his ideas. My perception of my diagnosis changed. The Holy Spirit made me feel better. The Holy Spirit blessed me. He taught me about health, diabetes, my Hemoglobin A1C (HbA1c) and labs. I used it to get my non-diabetic result. That's why this book is called GlucoSanity. Glucose and Sanity mean Glucose- normal blood sugar. Taber's Cyclopedic Medical Dictionary, 21st Edition F.A. Davis and Sanity - "Soundness of health or mind; mentally normal." The ability to think logically or rationally. So GlucoSanity is a normal blood sugar and Hemoglobin A1C level and soundness of health or mind mentally normal. The ability to think logically or rationally. To control glucose sanity, focus on the Holy Spirit. Let everything else become noise appearing in the background. The Holy Spirit takes the noise away.

When the noise is gone, you can hear the Holy Spirit's ideas to get your non-diabetic results.

Listening to the Holy Spirit, and Prayer

I talked to God about my diagnosis. I told him about the disease or condition. I listened to what he told me. I was already on the Daniel fast. The Daniel fast is a partial fast that is popular among Evangelical Protestants in North America, in which meat, wine and other rich foods are avoided in favor of vegetables and water for typically three weeks in order to be more sensitive to God. (Wikipedia).

CHAPTER II

The Daniel Fast

The influence of the Daniel Fast caused me to go beyond my feelings and to focus on the plan that God gave me before I was diagnosed with Diabetes. I wasn't supposed to take any medication. I was supposed to listen to my physician. I was supposed to do some of the things he asked me to do. He told me to lose weight. My physician didn't believe I could reverse it. He didn't believe that I could be healed. God can, does and is. I trusted the Holy Spirit. I lived out of my spirit. I acted on God-related thoughts given by the Holy Spirit; acting on those thoughts will produce revelation and give manifestation. It can be done.

Ignite Fast Day 3: Normal/Daniel Fast

FOOD FAST: Either water/clear fruit juice or DANIEL FAST

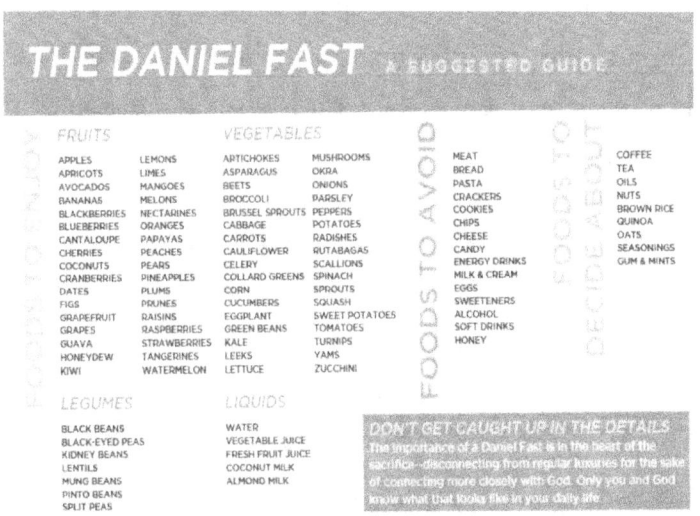

The Book of Joel in the Bible is a remarkable literary work. In once sense it is a dystopic and apocalyptic book that gives us a glimpse of the end of the world as we know it. But in another sense it is an optimistic book that renders an optimistic portrayal of how wonderful the world could be if we would simply worship and obey God. On one hand, the prophet Joel puts forth the concepts of judgment and times of testing upon God's people. But on the other hand, Joel, offers a 'cheat sheet' for times of testing and judgment and even offers hope that God will, indeed, not judge us if we only return to Him and make it right. Joel seems to make it clear that God's people have drifted too far from God and that terrible times are fast approaching on the horizon. But Joel also faithfully put's forth God's Heart towards His Own people based upon his intimate relationship with God.

"Even now," declares the Lord, "return to me with all your heart, with fasting and weeping and mourning." Rend your heart and not your garments. Return to the Lord your God, for he is gracious and compassionate, slow to anger and abounding in love, and he relents from sending calamity." Joel 2:12-13

Even now. Those two words indicate to us that it's never too late to repent. It's never too late to get right with God if we are doing so with our whole heart. In this text God uses a word twice. Return. He beckons His people to come back to Him although we've strayed. God also offers a key to what fasting is all about. Turning down our plate is an exercise of refocusing our attention upon God's Voice rather than our own basic needs. Fasting is also a means of self- assessment. It affords us increased time and space to look inwardly and determine where we are hurting, wounded or sad. The Hebrews addressed in this text were prone to grand gesturing in their religious lives. If they knew they'd offended God, they might throw dust on their heads and tear their (inexpensive) garments as a show of grief over their sin. God grew tired of such showy religious displays. He told them 'Rend your hearts and not your garments'. What are the symbolic religious gestures that you offer to God instead of your heart? Is it church attendance? Is it serving in your church? Is it your humanitarian efforts? Is it staying in a loveless marriage? We all have religious gestures that make us feel pious. But God says, Even now. After all of your gestures and religious exercises He simply wants you. Your heart. Your tears. Your attention. Your return to His Presence. I believe that if we obey this passage, we can experience breakthrough unlike we've ever seen.

Even now.

https://www.careviewcommunitychurch.org/single-post/2020/02/27/ignite-fast-day-3-normaldaniel-fast

CHAPTER III

The Diagnosis of Diabetes from my Physician

I went to an appointment with my physician, I gave the nurse a urine specimen. My urine was negative for glucose and infection. The nurse checked my weight, blood pressure, pulse, and temperature. I had a physical and an eye examination. I passed the physical examination. My vision was 20/20. I went to the laboratory to have my Hemoglobin A1C drawn. Someone called me to schedule an appointment with my physician to discuss my labs (Hemoglobin A1C). My physician told me I had diabetes. He talked to me about medication, losing weight, a follow up appointment and redrawing labs. I didn't want to take any medication. I knew I could get a non-diabetic result without taking medication. The Holy Spirit talked to me about getting a non-diabetic result without taking medication after

I was diagnosed with diabetes. My physician told me if my blood sugar was over 180, I needed medication. I scheduled an appointment to see if my urine was negative for glucose, and infection. To check my blood pressure, pulse, and temperature. I also wanted to see my laboratory results after my physician received them. He examined my feet during the physical exam. My physician talked to me; he told me I needed to lose 30lbs. In 3 to 4 months. He said the medication would help me lose weight. I didn't want any medication, he disagreed with me. The Holy Spirit led me not to take any medication. I was already on the Daniel fast. He said it would have been worse if I wasn't on it.

CHAPTER IV

Feelings - Shock, Overwhelmed, Hopeful

I felt shocked. My blood sugar and Hemoglobin A1C levels were abnormal. I was overwhelmed. My physician told me I had diabetes. This was unreal. What he told me about my Hemoglobin A1C, medication and weight loss was going through my mind. The Holy Spirit helped me to think logically and rationally. I knew he could heal me. I knew he would help me. I had to think about what the Holy Spirit told me instead of what my physician told me, so I would not lose hope. I went to my car and prayed. I left all the shock, overwhelm, and hopelessness in my physician's office. I felt hopeful because I knew Jesus could heal anything. After that, I went to the health food store.

CHAPTER V

A TRIP TO THE HEALTH FOOD STORE WHEAT GRASS, KIDNEY & LIVER DETOX TEAS

After I left my Primary Care Physician's office, I went to the health food store. I went to the health bar. The person made me 3 wheat grass shots. They had wheat grass and organic apple juice in them. I bought kidney and liver detox teas. I drank them at different times to change the disease or condition. I still go to the health food store to get wheat grass and other products for my health (smoothies, snacks, food, etc.). My body didn't know the difference between good carbs and bad carbs.

White/ brown

Rice

Bread

Pasta

They acted the same way in my body. I didn't switch from white to brown. I didn't eat them. I was already on the Daniel fast. I took 3 shots of wheat grass, detoxed my kidneys, and liver.

CHAPTER VI

Take everything to God in prayer, eating, exercise, etc. Eating, Exercise, Blood Sugars, Water Intake, nutritional shakes, reading books about diabetes, Praying, Taking Communion and weighing myself.

Take everything to God in prayer; ask him what you should eat. Get information from your Primary Care Physician about diabetes. You can also get information about what you should eat from a Registered Dietician. Ask God what kind of exercise you should do. It might be walking, Latin dance or aerobics. Ask your Primary Care Physician when and how often you should check your blood sugar. Drink a lot of water. Drink nutritional shakes, read books about diabetes, pray, and take communion every morning. Weigh yourself at the same time (with or without clothing and shoes) once a week. Wear the same thing. I weighed myself without clothing. I put my results in my journal. I took everything to God in prayer. I asked God what I should eat. I drank nutritional shakes. I eat lean white meat, snacks, fruit, raw and cooked vegetables, and sometimes peanut butter cookies. I got information about diabetes from my Primary Care Physician, television programs, a Registered Dietician, and my nursing education. I checked my blood sugar every morning. I drank water per the Holy Spirit's leading. I read books about diabetes. I prayed. I drank and ate per the Holy Spirit's leading. I took communion every morning. I weighed myself once a week. I continued to follow the Holy Spirit's lead. I prayed before I started, while I was listening to the Holy Spirit's plan, and then he gave me his plan. I followed the plan the Holy Spirit gave me to get my non-diabetic result. I prayed during the journey/ battle. I prayed after it. I continue to pray. Exercise even if you don't feel like it. I continue to pray. Exercise even if you don't feel like exercising after you wake up, exercise before you go to bed. I did 100 crunches before I got out of bed because if I didn't, I might not do them. I did 100 crunches before I got out of bed because abdominal fat affects your Hemoglobin A1C. Crunches brought my Hemoglobin A1C down. I weighed myself without clothing when I got out of bed. Walking wasn't working so I did Latin dance workouts when I started exercising. I did one workout, then I did two. I did a routine of 30 minutes a day at home. I did aerobics and rode my stationary bike while I was watching TV to exercise lower/ large muscle groups. I did quick results workouts. My blood sugar was going down. I checked my blood sugar every morning before I ate breakfast. I drank a 16.9 oz bottle of water before I drank a nutritional shake, and before bed. I drank nutritional shakes for snacks. I drank water after the nutritional shakes and before I went to bed. I drank nutritional shakes for lunch. I eat dinner. I read books about diabetes. I talked to God, listened to what he told me to do, and did it. I prayed before my diagnosis. I prayed during my diagnosis and I prayed after my diagnosis. I prayed without ceasing.

CHAPTER VII

The plans the Holy Spirit gave to me

The Holy Spirit gave a plan that included having faith, listening to him, receiving a diagnosis of diabetes, my feelings, a trip to the health food store, taking everything to God in prayer (eating, exercise etc.). Tips (eating, health), notes, and knowledge. I needed to have faith. I would not be a diabetic. I went to my Primary Care Physician's office for an appointment to get my urine, blood pressure, temperature and fasting blood sugar checked. My Primary Care Physician drew my blood to have my Hemoglobin A1C checked. The nurse called me to make an appointment to discuss my lab results with my Primary Care Physician. The nurse checked my fasting blood sugar. It was normal. We were happy. I waited for my Primary Care Physician to talk to me. God did it again!!!

The nurse weighed me. I lost more weight than my Primary Care Physician said I had to. He discussed my fasting, blood sugar, weight, and Hemoglobin A1C results with me. They were normal. He was happy. He asked me how I did it. I told him Jesus did it and I told him about some of the plans the Holy Spirit gave me. He said people don't want to do what needs to be done. They'd rather take medication. I learned tips about eating and health from the Holy Spirit, my Primary Care Physician, the health food store, Christian programs, and public health programs on TV about diabetes. The The Holy Spirit gave me some notes that helped me win my war against diabetes.

CHAPTER VIII

My Journal

DIET

I drank water after prayer and getting up. I exercised. I ate ¾ cup of heart healthy cereal, fat free milk which I added to my cereal. I drank 1 cup of orange juice and I drank 1 cup of unsweetened coffee for breakfast. I drank 1 cup of fat free milk for a snack. I drank a nutritional shake for lunch. I ate the baked chicken breast, broccoli (cooked), spinach (raw), and a cup of watermelon for dinner. I eat this most of the time. I also drank unsweetened Jasmine tea, herbal tea, and green tea. I drank grapefruit juice, lemon water, and water. I eat nutritional bars, cheese, 1 cup of popcorn popped in olive oil with salt added, fruit, rice cakes, green beans, eggs, onions, celery, grilled chicken, salad (dark leaf greens), cucumbers, bell peppers, olive oil based salad dressing, chicken thighs (baked or grilled), turkey, baked sandwich meat with no nitrates, and whole wheat bread.

WATER

I drank water per leading of the Holy Spirit. I drank 1 bottle (16.9 oz.) of water before breakfast lunch and dinner. I drank 5 bottles of water after prayer, and praise. Doing what the Holy Spirit tells you to do/his thoughts will Produce Revelation and Give Manifestation. I drank 6 bottles of water that day. I put the bottles of water on my table to make sure I drank them. I didn't drink anything after I drank my water.

WEIGHT REGIMEN

My Primary Care Physician told me I needed to lose 30lbs. I did 100 crunches before I got out of bed. I did one 15-minute Latin dance workout, then I did two 15-minute Latin dance workouts. I walked 1 mile a day (walking workout). My blood sugar wasn't normal. I stopped doing the walking workout. I started doing 30 minute aerobic workouts. 15 minutes- 30-minute Latin dance workouts, 30 minutes- 1hour dance workouts, riding my stationary bike or the Holy Spirit. Sometimes

I would ride at least 3 miles before I knew it because I was watching TV. I did line dancing workouts, yoga, abdominal workouts, belly dancing, and other workouts. I would do 100 crunches before I got out of bed, a 15-minute Latin dance workout, ride my stationary bike per the Holy Spirit's leading. I did another workout on the 6th day. I rested on the 7th day. I didn't continue to do this, but I still workout. My weight was 202lbs. I lost more than 30lbs.

CHAPTER IX

My Journal (Diary)

My blood sugars, diet, water, weight regimen, and weight loss results are in my journal/ diary.
Save for my MD office - 05/17/11 Blood Sugar 112

*My Hemoglobin A1C was 6.1

Blood Sugars/ Finger sticks

03/25/2011 - 171	04/24/2011 - 104
03/26/2011 - 161	04/25/2011 - 107
03/27/2011 - 144	04/26/2011 - 117
03/28/2011 - 161	04/27/2011 - 107
03/29/2011 - 146	04/28/2011 - 112
03/30/2011 - 149	04/29/2011 - 114
03/31/2011 - 125	04/30/2011 - 101

04/01/2011 - 119	05/01/2011 - 92
04/02/2011 - 142	05/02/2011 - 80
04/03/2011 - 125	05/03/2011 - 116
04/04/2011 - 125	05/04/2011 - 92
04/05/2011 - 144	05/05/2011 - 89
04/06/2011 - 109	05/06/2011 - 79
04/07/2011 - 95	05/07/2011 - 92
04/08/2011 - 108	05/08/2011 - 118
04/09/2011 - 112	05/09/2011 - 104
04/10/2011 - 108	05/10/2011 - 116
04/11/2011 - 123	05/11/2011 - 109
04/12/2011 - 108	05/12/2011 - 111
04/13/2011 - 104	05/13/2011 - 104
04/14/2011 - 105	05/14/2011 - 100
04/15/2011 - 111	05/15/2011 - 139
04/16/2011 - 116	05/16/2011 - 124
04/17/2011 - 132	05/17/2011 - 112
04/18/2011 - 106	
04/19/2011 - 100	
04/20/2011 - 110	
04/21/2011 - 119	
04/22/2011 - 122	
04/23/2011 - 111	

CHAPTER X

The end of a journey/ battle – Weight, Blood Pressure, Pulse, Temperature, Respirations, Urinalysis and other Laboratory Results

I went to my follow-up appointment. The nurse weighed me. I weighed more than 30lbs less than I did when she weighed me before my first physical exam. My blood pressure, pulse, temperature, respirations, urinalysis, and laboratory results were normal. My finger stick was normal. My Hemoglobin A1C was normal. I did not have to do finger sticks every day. I was so happy. My nurse was happy. My Primary Care Physician was happy. He was surprised. Jesus helped me. My Primary Care Physician talked to me about my Hemoglobin A1C and it was 6.1. It was the end of a journey/ battle. I drank water before my follow-up appointment.

CHAPTER XI

TIPS

1. Eat spinach like chips – on breaks, and in salads.

2. Don't add sugar to coffee.

3. Bring your fasting blood sugar down by putting cinnamon in drinks, coffee, smoothies etc.

4. Know what makes your blood sugar rise.

5. Keep a food diary/ journal.

6. Put your blood sugar in it so you will know what makes your blood sugar go up and down.

7. Put what you eat in your food diary/ journal each day.

8. Look at the food diary/ journal each day. The holy Spirit will lead you.

9. Take your fasting blood sugar daily.

10. If you want health (life) eat something alive everyday (fruit and vegetables)

11. Drink lots of water.

12. Don't put sugar or sugar substitutes in your beverages.

13. If you're not going to eat your vegetables. Drink them.

14. Put spinach, unsweetened coffee, almond milk, ice, a nutritional supplement and cinnamon in a blender then drink it.

15. Sometimes I put fruit, peanut butter, flax seeds, chia seeds and fruit juice in my smoothies.

16. I drank a small amount of orange juice after my first 30- minute workout.

CHAPTER XII

Key Points

1. Start each day with crunches.

2. End your day with water.

3. Monitor yourself (Fasting Blood Sugar).

4. Take communion daily.

5. Exercise 6 days per week.

6. Weigh yourself (with or without clothes) once a week.

7. Don't eat after your last workout.

8. You will be hungry.

9. Check the labels on the back of food, drinks, vitamins, etc. because I was surprised that frozen foods, vitamins and supplements had sugar in them.

CHAPTER XIII

Knowledge

1. Have faith.

2. Pray

3. Fast

4. Listen to what your physician says, talk to the Holy Spirit about it, and do what he says.

5. Talk to the Holy Spirit about your feelings.

6. Go to the health food store.

7. Take everything to God (eating, exercise, etc...)

8. The Holy Spirit will give you plans for your life.

9. Eat spinach, salads, fruit, eggs, cheese (non-processed), and vegetables (raw & cooked).

10. Drink protein and nutritional shakes/smoothies.

11. Write in your journal (blood sugar, water intake, weight etc…)

12. Win your journey/ battle with diabetes.

NOTES

www.ingramcontent.com/pod-product-compliance
Lightning Source LLC
LaVergne TN
LVHW010612070526
838199LV00063BA/5146